BAD KITTY
Camp Daze

NICK BRUEL

A NEAL PORTER BOOK
ROARING BROOK PRESS
NEW YORK

For Jim, Catherine, Zoe, and Astrid

Library of Congress Control Number: 201794447

ISBN: 978-1-62672-885-1

Our books may be purchased in bulk for promotional, educational, or business use. Please contact your local bookseller or the Macmillan Corporate and Premium Sales Department at (800) 221-7945 ext. 5442 or by e-mail at MacmillanSpecialMarkets@macmillan.com.

First edition 2018
Printed in the United States of America by LSC Communications, Harrisonburg, Virginia
1 3 5 7 9 10 8 6 4 2

• CONTENTS •

•CHAPTER ONE•
ONE FINE AFTERNOON

Good morning, Kitty!

Or perhaps I should say, "Good afternoon," seeing as it's 3:00 pm and morning ended hours ago.

Kitty, I know you can get pretty ornery if you don't get your usual 22 hours of sleep.

For that matter, I've seen you get ornery if your ice is too cold or if your water is too wet or if the sky is too blue. Sigh. Regardless, it's time to get up.

Besides, your breakfast is ready, and I have a really, really, really BIG surprise for you today!

8

Sorry, Kitty. That wasn't the surprise. Are you okay? Puppy has been waiting patiently all day to play with you, and I guess he got a little excited when he saw you were finally up. The really, really, really BIG surprise is . . .

Sorry again, Kitty. That wasn't the surprise either. Baby has been waiting patiently all day to play with you, too.

Are you sure you're okay? That's twice now that you've landed on your head.

Anyway, the really, really, really BIG surprise is . . .

Sorry again, Kitty. Are you okay? That was the mailman with a special delivery.

And the good news is that the delivery was for YOU! Why don't you open it?

15

It's a BRAND-NEW collar with a cool tag that has YOUR name on it! Isn't it COOL?! Isn't it AWESOME?! This will help if you ever get lost. All of the really cool cats are wearing them nowadays. That's what the salesman told me. All of your cat friends are going to be super-crazy jealous!

Put it on, Kitty! Now you look AWESOME. Totally COOL! Really GROOVY! Do cats still say "groovy"? Anyway, you look . . . uh-oh.

Oh, dear. They misspelled your name. It says "Katie" and not "Kitty." Oops. I guess that's my fault for ordering it over the phone.

But guess what, Kitty? The collar wasn't your really, really, really BIG surprise either! The surprise is that we ordered way too much Chinese food last night.

And you can have the leftovers for breakfast!

There's chicken fried rice and beef lo mein and duck chow fun and shrimp with broccoli and scallops with mixed vegetables and fried dumplings and steamed dumplings and Shanghai dumplings and egg rolls and spring rolls and . . . and . . .

AND IT'S ALL YOURS, KITTY!

Bon appétit!

20

21

Oh dear.

What a mess.

Sorry about that, Kitty. I'll clean this up and get your usual breakfast: a can of gray chicken-flavored paste with green bits.

25

27

•CHAPTER TWO•
ONE WEEK LATER

Hi, Puppy. You've been playing with Kitty a lot these past few days. But now you look exhausted. Why don't you lie down and take a nice, long nap?

30

KITTY! STOP THAT!

I'm thrilled that you and Puppy are suddenly getting along so well, but you've been playing with him nonstop for about a week now. He's turning into a nervous wreck. Just leave him alone for a little while and let him rest.

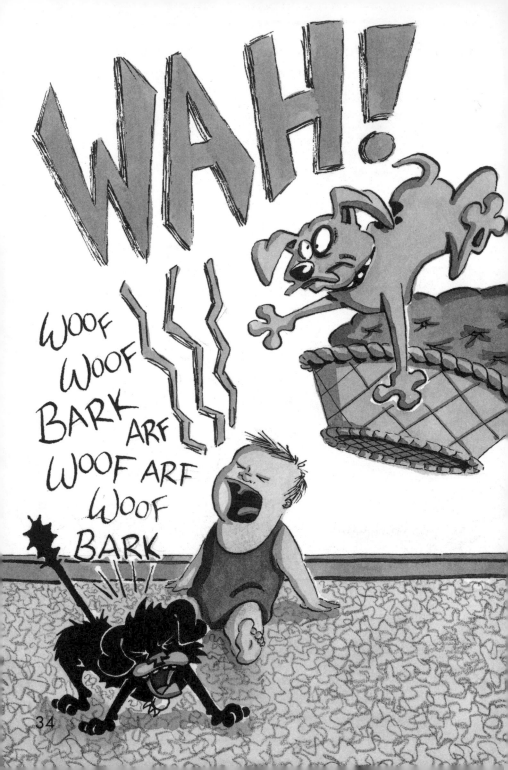

34

Wow, Puppy. You look pretty stressed out. Maybe you need a vacation. I think you need to go somewhere to relax and just be a dog.

But where? Hmmmmmmm . . .

Hey! Check it out! This could be the answer to your problems, Puppy! It's an advertisement for a new dog camp—a place where dogs can go for the weekend and get rid of their stress.

Is your Terrier tense?
Is your Poodle pooped?
Is your Hound harried?
Is your Sheepdog shaky?
Is your Bishon Frise frazzled?

What your dog needs
is a weekend at
**UNCLE MURRAY'S
CAMP FOR
STRESSED-OUT DOGS**
(No Goofy Cats Allowed)

Your dog will have a grand old time
fetching and swimming and hiking and
sleeping under the stars in a bucolic,
natural setting perfect for your pooch.

So, what do you say, Puppy? Feel like going to camp for a couple of days to try and relax?

Huh? What about YOU, Kitty? Sorry. This is a camp for dogs only. You are not a dog. You're a CAT, you silly thing.

Besides, why would you need to go to camp anyway? You don't have any stress. You don't have any chores or responsibilities. You sleep through most of the day. You don't even have to get your own food and water.

Your entire life is like an endless summer vacation on a cruise ship that's shaped like this living room.

Let's go, Puppy. I'll help you pack.

•CHAPTER THREE•
CAMP!

Here we are, Puppy! I hope you're ready for two days of fun, rest, and relaxation.

Don't forget your duffel bag! You'll need this.

It's funny, though. Your bag feels a lot lighter than when I packed it earlier today. Oh well.

52

54

57

63

UNCLE MURRAY'S FUN FACTS

WHY ARE DOGS BETTER AT FETCHING THAN CATS?

How is that relevant here?

Not all dogs like to play fetch. But those that do can become obsessed with the game.

Why do dogs like to play fetch so much?
Built into a dog's brain is the instinct to fetch: to hunt and chase and capture smaller animals. Instinct is the knowledge an animal is born with that helps it to survive. No one teaches a bird how to fly. It just knows. No one teaches a dog how to fetch. It just knows. But without any smaller animals around, a stick or a tennis ball will do.

But cats are hunters, too. So why don't they play fetch?

A few of them do. Cats are natural born fetchers. Their mouths are perfectly designed to grab small items and animals and then carry them around. Think of a mother cat and how she will pick up and carry her kittens.

So why don't cats play fetch like dogs?

Cats just aren't generally as playful with people as dogs are. One reason is because cats like to conserve their energy. It's why they sleep so much. Their instinct tells them to rest as much as possible so they'll have the energy to hunt later.

Another reason is because they tend to be loners. Cats will be affectionate with their owners, but tend not to play with them the same way dogs do. This means that cats will often chase a toy you throw, but they'll rarely pick it up and bring it back.

More playful. More energetic. This all just goes to prove that dogs are better than cats. So, there.

What's the first swim stroke kids learn? It's the dog paddle! Not the giraffe paddle or the rhinoceros paddle or the kitty paddle. The dog paddle.

Do all dogs know how to swim?
Not all, but most dogs instinctively know how to swim. If a dog is put in deep water, its legs will begin trotting like a horse, moving in a motion like it's walking quickly. This will help the dog stay afloat. But you still have to be careful. Many dogs will try swimming, but just won't be able to float at all, so you have to be very careful before putting any dog in water that goes above its head.

Do cats also know how to swim?

They do, but they don't like it. A cat's instinct tells it to hunt for food on the ground and in the woods and in the trees, which is why they're better at climbing than dogs.

But the really big reason dogs generally like to swim more than cats is because cats HATE TO GET WET.

Like it or not, hairless cats, like yours truly, NEED a bath at least once a week.

A cat's fur is finer and softer than a dog's, so it doesn't dry as quickly. This means that if a cat gets soaking wet, it will stay wet for a long time and that can be very uncomfortable.

Dogs swim. Cats don't. Dogs win. So, there.

Once there was a brave dog. Swell guy. Smart. Handsome, too. No trouble with the ladies. Smelled nice.

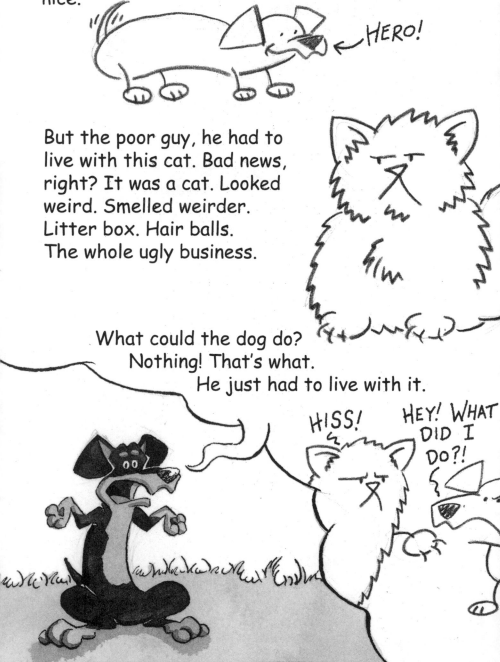

But the poor guy, he had to live with this cat. Bad news, right? It was a cat. Looked weird. Smelled weirder. Litter box. Hair balls. The whole ugly business.

What could the dog do? Nothing! That's what. He just had to live with it.

But then, one day—just when the dog thought things couldn't get worse, they got worse. WAY WORSE. One day, it was as if the cat EXPLODED! All of a sudden, there were these teeny, little cats all over the place. Plus, the original.

They were in the food. They were in the water.

YEESH!

TOBY

They were on the bed. They were on the couch.

Did I mention the food? They were in the FOOD, for crying out loud!

WHAT THE...?

NOT AGAIN!

TOBY

The dog did his absolute best to endure this whole gruesome situation. But these things, they had no sense of boundaries!

They played with his ears!

HEY! CUT THAT OUT!

QUIT IT!

They played with his tail!

They tormented him day and night!

Soon the poor dog had no choice but to go completely . . .

INSANE!

Once there was a dog. She was a very good dog. She chewed up a shoe a couple of times, but only because the shoe was asking for it. She rarely had an accident in the house. She was a good dog.

GOOD DOG

BAD SHOE

Then, one day, the dog's owner brought a horrible creature into the house. It was orange and scaly and had a huge flat tail. The poor dog knew immediately it could only be a WATERCAT!

The worst feature of the watercat was its eyes—its huge, cold empty eyes that stared deep into the dog's soul! All day, every day, the watercat would float about in its home staring, STARING at the dog.

It stared at the dog when she was drinking out of the toilet, (which the dog knew she wasn't supposed to do). It stared at the dog when she sat on the sofa (which the dog knew she wasn't supposed to be on).

It stared at the dog when she was having an argument with the shoe (which the dog knew she wasn't supposed to do).

That's when the dog realized that the watercat was placed there by her owners to watch her every move and report her every crime! It was enough to make the poor dog go completely

INSANE!

103

105

My 10 Greatest Fears

10- Chickens go extinct.

9- Worldwide beef shortage.

8- Vacuum cleaners grow wings.

7- My tail really is a snake.

6- President Puppy.

5- The mailman tries to eat me.

4- The vet tries to eat me.

3- That cat in the mirror uses my litter box.

2- Baths.

1- Waking up in the woods surrounded by dogs.

WHY DO CATS LIKE CATNIP?

This is really not a good time!

Only about 50 percent of cats actually respond to catnip, but for those that do—watch out!

What is catnip?
Catnip is a type of mint that contains nepetalactone, a chemical which can have a powerful effect on cats.

CRAZY   SNIFF

MELLOW   BURP

How do cats respond to it?
Cats can either sniff catnip or eat it. Cats who smell catnip have been known to roll in it, rub their faces in it, and can sometimes become very hyper and energetic. Interestingly, when a cat eats catnip, the opposite can happen: The cat can become very mellow and sleepy.

Why does this happen?
To be honest, even scientists don't know exactly why nepetalactone can have such a dramatic effect on a

cat's behavior. All they
is that this chemical can n
a cat go bonkers for as l
as ten minutes to as much c
two hours. This chemica
has even been known to
affect big cats like leopards and tigers.

Does catnip affect dogs?
Dogs don't go crazy over the scent of
catnip like cats do, but they will get
sleepy if they eat it. Some people will
put a few catnip leaves in a dog's water
bowl to help it calm down.

I smell licorice!

Is there such a thing as "dognip"?
The smell of anise seed, the same herb
that flavors licorice, can make some dogs
go completely nuts in the same way catnip
can affect cats. But you have to be careful.
The ASPCA warns that too much anise can
really bother a dog's stomach.

Chemicals. Licorice. ASPCA. Got it!
Just tell that cat to slow down!

Ho . . . **huff** . . . holy . . . **huff puff** . . . h[o]
salami . . . **gasp!** Thank you for stopping. **Cho**[.]
Cat, I don't know how you got here or why yo[u]
would even want to be here, but the woods can[']
be a dangerous place. It's going to be dark soon,
so we should go back to the camp and figure out
what to do with you in the morning.

You have
claws,
sharp like
knives! You have
teeth, strong like
spikes! You have breath,
powerful like garlic left outside
on a hot day! No mere man can
frighten you! No mere
beast can defeat you!

Tell me who you are!

MEOW

CHAPTER NINE

MEANWHILE . . .

147

Seriously! She may be a cat. She may be goo[d?] [She?] may be the source of all our problems, but w[hen we?] needed her most, she came through for me[.]

Something kind of beautiful happened today. I ran after Kitty to keep her safe. She saved me from a bear. You dogs found us when we were lost. We all looked out for each other! Maybe it's time we all paid more attention to those things that unify us instead of fighting over the things that divide us.

CHAPTER ELEVEN

HOME AGAIN

WELCOME HOME, PUPPY!
It's great to see you. You look much more like
your old self. I think that camp really helped.

KITTY! Where have YOU been the past couple o
days? Did you get lost? And what happened to your
brand-new collar? Did you lose it already? Great. Oh
well. I suppose it wasn't all that useful if you had it
and STILL got lost.

The important thing is that you're both home safe
and sound.

ou guys look tired. Why don't you two go lie down and have a nice rest while I put together some food for you.